THE
COW
ABDUCTION
CHRONICLES

A MOOLOT CRISIS

IT IS THE YEAR 5051 AND A
deep-space planet known as ΩÏ√E
is in trouble! A species called
Moolots inhabit this far-out world,
and they have just made an
alarming discovery: their planet is
dying—as in, could become com-
pletely uninhabitable in the time

it takes you to read this book!

You see, Moolots require methane not only to live and breathe, but to power their ships. It's a resource that was once abundant on their planet. Recently the scientists of ΩÏ√E discovered that the planet's formerly methane-rich atmosphere is being eaten away by a foreign entity called lactose, creating an excessive amount of toxic gas, which could eventually cause the whole planet to erupt. The Moolots must find a new source of methane that's lactose-tolerant, and they need to find it *soon*.

There is one planet that can help them—one harboring an abundant source of methane. But the Moolots will have to travel into a faraway galaxy to obtain it. The planet is called Earth, which has very unpredictable, wasteful creatures living on it. The Moo-lots have always maintained a healthy distance to keep their existence a secret.

A MOST DANGEROUS MISSION

—

THUS, PLANET Ω Ï √E HAS A VERY dangerous mission to tackle, and right now they only have enough methane to send a single ship. Let's examine the transcript of the conversation that led to this historic undertaking…

CORPORAL FLAT: *Commander Tip, we have just been briefed that our planet is below threshold on methane. A new source must be located immediately.*

COMMANDER TIP: Flat, why should I care if methane levels are low or high? I have more important things to consider.

FLAT: *Why should you care? We need this gas for our ships in order to travel through time and* multiple dimensions. Heck, we need this gas to breathe! Everyone has been talking about this crisis. Where have you been?

TIP: Okay, okay, let's start looking into a way to get a new source, and we must conserve what we have now. Flat, you sound like you are ready to take on this crucial mission.

FLAT: Yes, sir, I know just where we might find more methane:

Earth, a planet I know from my travels. Earth has a dangerous overabundance of greenhouse gases. We'd be helping Earthlings by taking some of their methane! Getting there and back isn't going to be easy, but I've visited other planets in the same galaxy and I can do this!

TIP: Why are you still here? Go, go, go!

Flat loads up the resources he needs, says goodbye to his family, and in the blink of an eye, is headed straight through a wormhole and multiple dimensions. Just as it becomes uncertain if his fuel supply will hold out, Earth comes into view. To Flat's shock, his spaceship begins recharging immediately as he enters the planet's stratosphere. Amazing!

Upon landing, Flat begins investigating this strange new land. He comes up with a plan to remain unseen by Earthlings while creating circular markings in fields that track where he has been and contain discreetly hidden notes about his discoveries. He spends a couple of days endlessly researching and observing the creatures of Earth. One place in particular seems to have an abnormality…

SOMEWHERE IN NEW JERSEY

—

FLAT FOLLOWS THE HEIGHTENED
amount of gas coming from a
field. To his surprise, the source is a
spotted beast that does not seem
to be the least bit bothered by his
presence. "I must learn more about
this creature," Flat says to himself.
He quickly swoops in closer with his

spaceship and starts the abduction process—also known as the Alternative Passenger Boarding Procedure in the spaceship's manual.

The spotted creature looks up at the spaceship lights, unfazed, and continuing to graze the land around him. The warm light then gently lifts its new passenger up higher and higher until the boarding procedure has been successfully completed.

Flat is then able to inspect the creature closely using the ship's information probe—a Moolot-designed masterpiece. The probe begins the process of analyzing the subject's DNA structure, health history, species, and level of methane emissions. It even reveals memories!

While Corporal Flat is waiting for the results, he notices a tiny marking on the subject's neck.

It's the number fifty-two on Earth, but it translates to "Fifi" in Flat's language. Flat records the marking as the creature's name in his logbook.

The results of the analysis are soon in. This beautiful creature is a bovine—specifically, a cow. Upon close review of the charts, Flat sees that Fifi is in perfect health. Better yet, the cow's methane readings are so high that they have almost destroyed his research equipment. Flat jumps for joy, but his work is not done yet.

Curious about Fifi's high methane readings, Corporal Flat decides to take a peek at the cow's memories. Most are of her eating grass, but the memories also give Flat a disturbing first-hand look at what it is like to be a cow on Earth. The corporal immediately finds new meaning

in his already-crucial mission. He
promises Fifi a better life before
yelling out loud, "It's go time! Are
you ready, girl?"

BACK TO
ΩÏ√E

—

FLAT SENDS A SIGNAL ALERTING
his home planet that he is on
his way back. He soothes Fifi,
telling her to hold on as the ride
might get a little crazy. Fifi is truly
unbothered, but lets out a few
moos before they blast off into
space. They travel back through

the wormhole and multiple dimensions again, but this time Flat's ship stays charged, apparently thanks to Fifi. The corporal is impressed with the power the cow has. He knows that his home planet is going to love her!

Finally arriving back home and reporting to the planet's central military base, Tip introduces Fifi to his fellow scientists, and they immediately start working to inspect the creature and manage her powers. They observe that the cow doesn't move much and seems to want to eat the ground.

One scientist pokes Fifi, releasing a loud gaseous eruption from the animal. Everything nearby is on the receiving end of a glorious breeze: a breath of fresh…methane! Hooray! "What are these things?" the scientist asks.

"I don't know," Flat replies, "but

I've witnessed Earthlings grope this creature's teats. They use the liquid produced to soak their morning cereal, despite causing what appears to be some major gastronomical disturbances. And, clearly, her methane readings are off the charts. If we can abduct other creatures like her from Earth, give them a humane life on ΩÏ√E, and harness their methane emissions, our planet will be saved!"

BOVINE-NIRVANA

—

FLAT IS AWARDED THE MEDAL of Flatulence in recognition of the outstanding success of his dangerous mission, and he is even promoted to General. The new general promptly starts his own squadron dedicated to finding and transporting cows

back to ΩÏ√E. His team trains and works together in visits to Earth hundreds of times a year. Over time, ΩÏ√E's methane levels return to normal: the planet has created a sustainable future!

The Moolots are so appreciative of Fifi and other cows' help that they make the bovine the official planet animal. Corporal Flat himself even successfully lobbies to change the planet name from ΩÏ√E to Bovine-Nirvana, the ultimate cow sanctuary in the universe.

All the while, Earthlings have no idea why their greenhouse gases are becoming less of a threat, or where their cows are going, for that matter. Little do they know, Moolots are always around them, from a safe distance.

At the end of this weird little story, two planets are saved. Back on Bovine-Nirvana, the

Moolots propose a cheers with a glass of their newest favorite beverage, milk.

(Let us hope it's lactose-free, for the sake of all!)

This book has been bound
using handcraft methods and
Smyth-sewn to ensure durability.

Designed by Ashley Todd.

Written by Matt Smiriglio.

Illustrated by Mario Zucca.